TAO TE CHING

LAO TZU

TAO TE CHING

THE BOOK OF MEANING AND LIFE

Translation by Richard Wilhelm
Translated into English
by H. G. Oswald

penguin books

PENGUIN BOOKS
Published by the Penguin Group
Penguin Books USA Inc., 375 Hudson Street,
New York, New York 10014, U.S.A.
Penguin Books Ltd, 27 Wrights Lane,
London W8 5TZ, England
Penguin Books Australia Ltd, Ringwood,
Victoria, Australia
Penguin Books Canada Ltd, 10 Alcorn Avenue,
Toronto, Ontario, Canada M4V 3B2
Penguin Books (N.Z.) Ltd, 182–190 Wairau Road,
Auckland 10, New Zealand

Penguin Books Ltd, Registered Offices:
Harmondsworth, Middlesex, England

This translation first published in Great Britain
as an Arkana Paperback by Routledge & Kegan Paul, 1985
Published in Arkana (imprint of Penguin Books Ltd) 1990
Published in Penguin Books 1995

ISBN 0 14 60.0085 4

Printed in the United States of America

CONTENTS

Preface

Experts in Chinese studies will agree that anyone undertaking a new translation of Lao Tzo's *Tao Te Ching* must put forward a good case for doing so. For no other Chinese literary text has attracted as much attention and as many attempts at translation in the past hundred years or so. The mysterious qualities and difficulties of the text are a challenge to thought and reflection. And as the *Tao Te Ching* is a literary work which is not always understood even by Chinese scholars, the ambitious sinologue finds himself all the more tempted to undertake the task. For if many Chinese men of letters are not up to it, he feels he has a right—if he cannot do better—at least to misunderstand it. This justification for an individual interpretation may go even further still. It has been said that more than one uninhibited rendering of the ancient sage's work has been published that is based not on the Chinese text, but on an intuitive interpretation of what others—less inspired—had failed to grasp in terms of philosophical depth in their English or French versions of the text. Strangely enough, the psychological kinship often seems to be so close that the ancient Chinese sage will often show a remarkable sympathy with the thought of his respective translator.

In view of this profusion of translations, the reader may ask with good reason why yet another one should be added to their number. I have been encouraged to publish this new version for two reasons. The first constitutes the underlying principle of this edition. Among the many documents of Chinese religion and philosophy, this brief text, the source of so much influence, cannot be ignored—even if only the most important parts of it are to be represented, as is intended here. In addition, by placing the text in its true historical and philosophical context a new light will be cast on it, capable of clarifying and rectifying much that appears strange or incomprehensible when it is viewed in isolation. The second reason is that it seems a good idea that after so many modern interpretations the ancient Chinese sage himself should have his say.

The literature on Lao Tzu is considerable. In working through it, I found the number of new things that have been said about him dismally small in proportion to the sheer quantity of what has been written. In fact, one discovers that certain common elements find their way from one book into all subsequent ones, partly by acknowledgment, and partly by rejection. Given this situation, there seemed to be no point in compiling yet another text from the existing ones: it seemed far more desirable to draw on Chinese literature itself. For this reason both the translation of the *Tao Te Ching* and the commentary on the text* are based on Chinese sources throughout.

---

*This Penguin 60s edition contains only Wilhem's translation of the text itself. His extensive introduction, commentary, and notes are available in the complete Penguin Arkana edition of this book.

At the same time, however, none of the more important issues in the continuing discussion of the Tao Te Ching is thought to have been neglected. In certain circumstances even silence is a kind of recognition, particularly where the available space does not allow the translator to go into detail, and prove his own point of view. It is significant that new discoveries are made almost every day where Lao Tzu is concerned, and it might have been tempting to offer yet another one. Instead, I have put forward many points here which may appear old-fashioned to some. Other questions which one would have liked to pronounce on decisively have had to be left unresolved. But that is how things are in this world: one cannot satisfy everybody.

On the whole I owe many happy hours of contemplation to my work on this brief Chinese text, and if this attempt at a new translation brings the same pleasure to its readers it will not have been in vain.

I want to thank Dr. jur. Harald Gutherz, lecturer at the law faculty of the new German-Chinese College at Qingdao who has generously contributed to this edition by permitting the inclusion of the fairy tale, stylised by him, in the commentary on section 80, and Friedrich Boie, schoolteacher at Thorn, who was kind enough to do the proof-reading.

—Richard Wilhelm
Qingdao, 1 December 1910

PART ONE: TAO

1

The TAO that can be expressed
is not the eternal TAO.
The name that can be named
is not the eternal name.
'non-existence' I call the beginning of Heaven and Earth.
'Existence' I call the mother of individual beings.
Therefore does the direction towards non-existence
lead to the sight of the miraculous essence,
the direction towards existence
to the sight of spatial limitations.
Both are one in origin
and different only in name.
In its unity it is called the secret.
The secret's still deeper secret
is the gateway through which all miracles emerge.

2

If all on earth acknowledge the beautiful as beautiful
then thereby the ugly is already posited.
If all on earth acknowledge the good as good

then thereby is the non-good already posited.
For existence and non-existence generate each other.
Heavy and light complete each other.
Long and Short shape each other.
High and deep convert each other.
Before and after follow each other.

Thus also is the Man of Calling.
He dwells in effectiveness without action.
He practises teaching without talking.
All beings emerge
and he does not refuse himself to them.
He generates and yet possesses nothing.
He is effective and keeps nothing.
When the work is done
he does not dwell with it.
And just because he does not dwell
he remains undeserted.

3

By not preferring the competent
one brings about that people do not quarrel.
By not treasuring precious things
one brings about that people do not steal.
By not displaying desirable things
one brings about that people's hearts are not confused.

Therefore the Man of Calling governs thus:
He empties their hearts and fills their bellies.

He weakens their will and strengthens their bones
and brings about that the people remain without knowledge
and without wishes,
and he takes care
that those who know dare not act.
He does the non-doing,
and thus everything falls into place.

4

TAO is forever flowing.
And yet it never overflows in its effectiveness.
It is an abyss like the ancestor of all things.
It mellows their acuity.
It dissolves their confusion.
It mitigates their brightness.
It unites itself with their dust.
It is deep and yet as if real.
I do not know whose son it is:
It seems to be earlier than God.

5

Heaven and Earth are not benevolent.
To them men are like straw dogs destined for sacrifice.
The Man of Calling is not benevolent.
To him men are like straw dogs destined for sacrifice.
The space between Heaven and Earth
is like a flute:

empty, and yet it does not collapse;
when moved more and more emerges from it.
But many words exhaust themselves on it.
It is better to guard the 'within'.

6

The spirit of the valley never dies.
It is called 'the female'.
The gateway of the dark female
is called 'the root of Heaven and Earth'.
Uninterrupted as though persistent
it is effective without effort.

7

Heaven is eternal and Earth lasting.
They are lasting and eternal
because they do not live for themselves.
Therefore can they live forever.

Thus also is the Man of Calling:
He disregards himself,
and his Self is increased.
He gives himself away
and his Self is preserved.
Is it not thus:
because he desires nothing as his own
his own is completed?

8

The highest benevolence is like water.
The benevolence of water is
to benefit all beings without strife.
It dwells in places which man despises.
Therefore it stands close to TAO.
In dwelling benevolence shows itself in place.
In thinking benevolence shows itself in depth.
In giving benevolence shows itself in love.
In speech benevolence shows itself in truth.
In ruling benevolence shows itself in order.
In working benevolence shows itself in competence.
In movement benevolence shows itself in timing.
He who does not assert himself
thereby remains free of blame.

9

To hold on to something and thereby make it overflow:
this is not worthwhile.
To make use of something and still keep it sharp:
this cannot be sustained for long.
A palace full of gold and diamonds
nobody can protect.
To be rich and titled and arrogant into the bargain:
this in itself attracts misfortune.
When the work is done it is time to withdraw:
this is the TAO of Heaven.

Can you educate your soul so that it encompasses the One
without dispersing itself?
Can you make your strength unitary
and achieve that softness
that makes you like a little child?
Can you cleanse your secret seeing
so that it becomes free of stain?
Can you love men and rule the state
so that you remain without knowledge?
Can you, when the gates of Heaven
open and close, be like the female bird?
Can you penetrate everything with your inner clarity and purity
without having need for action?
Generating and nourishing,
generating and not possessing,
being effective and not retaining,
increasing and not dominating: this is the secret Life.

Thirty spokes surround the hub:
In their nothingness consists the carriage's effectiveness.
One hollows the clay and shapes it into pots:
In its nothingness consists the pot's effectiveness.
One cuts out doors and windows to make the chamber:
In their nothingness consists the chamber's effectiveness.

Therefore: what exists serves for possession.
What does not exist serves for effectiveness.

12

The five colours blind men's eyes.
The five tones deafen men's ears.
The five flavours spoil men's palates.
Running and chasing make men's hearts mad.
Rare goods confuse men's ways.

Therefore the Man of Calling
works for the body's needs, not for the eye's.
He removes the other and takes this.

13

Grace is as shameful as a fright.
Honour is a great evil like the persona.
What does this mean: 'Grace is as shameful as a fright'?
Grace is something inferior.
One attains it, and one is as if frightened.
This is what is meant by 'Grace is as shameful as fright'.
What does this mean: 'Honour is a great evil like the persona'?
The reason I experience great evil is
that I have a persona.
If I have no persona:
What evil could I experience?

Therefore: whosoever honours the world in his persona
to him one may entrust the world.
Whosoever loves the world in his persona
To him one may hand over the world.

14

One looks for it and does not see it:
its name is 'seed'.
One listens for it and does not hear it:
its name is 'subtle'.
One reaches for it and does not feel it:
its name is 'small'.
These three cannot be separated,
therefore, intermingled they form the One.
Its highest is not light,
its lowest is not dark.
Welling up without interruption,
one cannot name it.
It returns again to non-existence.
This is called the formless form,
the objectless image.
This is called the darkly chaotic.
Walking towards it one does not see its face;
following it one does not see its back.
If one holds fast to the TAO of antiquity

in order to master today's existence

one may know the ancient beginning.
This means: TAO's continuous thread.

15

Those who in ancient times were competent as Masters
were one with the invisible forces of the hidden.
They were deep so that one cannot know them.
Because one cannot know them
therefore one can only painfully describe their exterior.
Hesitating, like one who crosses a river in winter,
cautious, like one who fears neighbours on all sides,
reluctant, like guests,
dissolving like ice that is melting,
simple like unworked matter:
broad they were, like the valley,
impenetrable to the eye they were like the turbid.
Who can clear up the turbid, little by little,
through stillness (as they did)?
Who can create stillness, little by little,
through duration (as they did)?
Whosoever guards this TAO
does not desire abundance.
For only because he has no abundance
therefore can he be modest,
avoid what is new
and attain completion

Create emptiness up to the highest!
Guard stillness up to the most complete.
Then all things may rise together.
I see how they return.
Things in all their multitude:
each one returns to its root.
Return to the root means stillness.
Stillness means return to fate.
Return to fate means eternity.
Cognition of eternity means clarity.
If one does not recognise the eternal
one falls into confusion and sin.
If one recognises the eternal
one becomes forbearing.
Forbearance leads to justice.
Justice leads to mastery.
Mastery leads to Heaven.
Heaven leads to TAO.
TAO leads to duration.
All one's life long one is not in danger.

If a wholly Great One rules
the people hardly know that he exists.
Lesser men are loved and praised,
10 still lesser ones are feared,

still lesser ones are despised.
How thoughtful one must be in what one says!
The work done, business takes its course,
and all people think:
'We are free.'

18

If the great TAO perishes
there will be morality and duty.
When cleverness and knowledge arise
great lies will flourish.
When relatives fall out with one another
there will be filial duty and love.
When states are in confusion
there will be faithful servants.

19

Put away holiness, throw away knowledge:
thus the people will profit a hundredfold.
Put away morality, throw away duty:
thus the people will return to filial duty and love.
Put away skilfulness, throw away gain,
and there will no longer be thieves and robbers.
In these three things
beautiful appearance is not enough.
Therefore take care that men have something to hold on to.
Show simplicity, hold fast to honesty!

Diminish selfishness, reduce desire!
Give up learnedness!
Thus you shall become free of sorrows.

20

Between 'definitely' and 'probably':
what difference is there?
Between 'good' and 'evil':
what difference is there?
What men honour one must honour.
O loneliness, how long will you last?
All men are so shining-bright
as if they were going to the great sacrificial feast,
as if they were climbing up the towers in spring.
Only I am so reluctant, I have not yet been given a sign:
like an infant, yet unable to laugh;
unquiet, roving as if I had no home.
All men have abundance,
only I am as if forgotten.
I have the heart of a fool: so confused, so dark.
Men of the world are shining, alas, so shining-bright;
only I am as if turbid.
Men of the world are so clever, alas, so clever;
only I am as if locked into myself,
unquiet, alas, like the sea,
turbulent, alas, unceasingly.
All men have their purpose,
only I am futile like a beggar.

I alone am different from all men:
But I consider it worthy
to seek nourishment from the Mother.

21

The substance of the great Life
completely follows TAO.
TAO brings about all things
so chaotically, so darkly.
Chaotic and dark
are its images.
Unfathomable and obscure in it
is the seed.
This seed is wholly true.
In it dwells reliability.
From ancient times to this day
we cannot make do without names
in order to view all things.
Whence do I know the nature of things?
Just through them.

22

What is half shall become whole.
What is crooked shall become straight.
What is empty shall become full.
What is old shall become new.

Whosoever has little shall receive.
Whosoever has much, from him shall be taken away.

Thus also is the Man of Calling:
he encompasses the One
and sets an example to the world.
He does not want to shine,
therefore will he be enlightened.
He does not want to be anything for himself,
therefore he becomes resplendent.
He does not lay claim to glory,
therefore he accomplishes works.
He does not seek excellence,
therefore he will be exalted.
Because whosoever does not quarrel
with him no-one in the world can quarrel.
What the ancients said: 'That which is half shall become
    full,'
is truly not an empty phrase.
All true completeness is summed up in it.

23

Use words sparingly,
then all things will fall into place.
A whirlwind does not last a whole morning.
A downpour of rain does not last a whole day.
And who works these?
Heaven and Earth.

What Heaven and Earth cannot do enduringly:
how much less can man do it?

Therefore if you set about your work with TAO
you will be at one in TAO with those who have TAO,
at one in Life with those who have Life,
at one in poverty with those who are poor.
If you are at one with them in TAO
those who have TAO will come to meet you joyfully.
If you are at one with them in Life
those who have Life will come to meet you joyfully.
If you are at one with them in poverty
those who are poor will come to meet you joyfully.
But where faith is not strong enough
there one is not believed.

24

Whosoever stands on tiptoe
does not stand firmly.
Whosoever stands with legs astride
will not advance.
Whosoever wants to shine
will not be enlightened.
Whosoever wants to be someone
will not become resplendent,
Whosoever glorifies himself
does not accomplish works.
Whosoever boasts of himself

will not be exalted.
For TAO he is like kitchen refuse and a festering sore.
And all the creatures loathe him.
Therefore: whosoever has TAO
does not linger with these.

25

There is one thing that is invariably complete.
Before Heaven and Earth were, it is already there:
so still, so lonely.
Alone it stands and does not change.
It turns in a circle and does not endanger itself.
One may call it 'the Mother of the World'.
I do not know its name.
I call it TAO.
Painfully giving it a name
I call it 'great'.
Great: that means 'always in motion'.
'Always in motion' means 'far away'.
'Far away' means 'returning'.
Thus TAO is great, Heaven is great, Earth is great,
and Man too is great.
There are in space four Great Ones,
and Man is one of them.
Man conforms to Earth.
Earth conforms to Heaven.
Heaven conforms to TAO.
TAO conforms to itself.

The weighty is the root of the light.
Stillness is the lord of restlessness.

Thus also is the Man of Calling.
He wanders all day
without discarding his heavy load.
Even when he has all the glory before his eyes
he remains satisfied in his loneliness.
How much less may the lord of the realm
take the world lightly in his person!
By taking it lightly one loses the root.
Through restlessness one loses mastery.

A good wanderer leaves no trace.
A good speaker has no need to refute.
A good arithmetician needs no abacus.
A good guard needs neither lock nor key—
and yet no-one can open what he guards.
A good binder needs neither string nor ribbon,
and yet no-one can untie what he has bound.
The Man of Calling always knows how to rescue men:
therefore, for him there are no abject men.
He always knows how to rescue things:
therefore for him there are no abject things
This means: living in clarity.

Thus good men are the teachers of the non-good,
and non-good men are the subject-matter of the good.
Whosoever does not cherish his teachers
and does not love his subject-matter:
for all his knowledge he would be in grave error.
This is the great secret.

Whosoever knows his maleness
and guards his femaleness:
he is the gorge of the world.
If he is the gorge of the world
eternal Life does not leave him
and he becomes again as a child.

Whosoever knows his purity
and guards his weakness
is an example to the world.
If he is an example to the world
eternal Life does not leave him
and he returns to the uncreated.

Whosoever knows his honour
and guards his shame:
he is the valley of the world.
If he is the valley of the world
he finds satisfaction in eternal Life

and returns to simplicity.

If simplicity is dispersed there will be 'useful' men.
If the Man of Calling practises it
he will be the lord of the servants.
Therefore: Great Design
has no need for pruning.

29

Conquering and handling the world:
I have experienced that this fails.
The world is a spiritual thing
which must not be handled.
Whosoever handles it destroys it,
whosoever wants to hold on to it loses it.
Now things run ahead, now they follow.
Now they blow warm, now they blow cold.
Now they are strong, now they are thin.
Now they are on top, now they topple.
Therefore the Man of Calling avoids
what is too intense, too much, too big.

30

Whosoever in true TAO helps a ruler of men
does not rape the world by use of arms,
for actions return onto one's own head.
Where armies have dwelt thistles and thorns grow.
Behind battles follow years of hunger.

Therefore the competent seeks only decision, nothing
   further.
He does not dare conquer by force.
Decision without boasting;
decision without glorifying;
decision without arrogance;
decision because it cannot be helped;
decision removed from force.

31

Weapons are instruments of bad omen:
all beings, I believe, loathe them.
Therefore, whosoever has the true TAO
does not want to know about them.
The noble man, in his ordinary life,
considers the left the place of honour.
In the art of warfare
the right is the place of honour.
Weapons are instruments of bad omen,
not instruments for the noble.
He uses them only when he cannot help it.
Quietness and peace are his highest values.
He gains victory but he does not rejoice in it.
Whosoever would rejoice in it
would, in fact, rejoice in the murder of men.
Whosoever would rejoice in the murder of men
cannot achieve his goal in the world.

In fortunate circumstances one considers the left the place of
   honour.
In unfortunate circumstances one considers the right place of
   honour.
The vice-commander stands to the left,
the supreme commander to the right.
This means: he takes his place
according to the rules for memorial services.
Killing men in great numbers
one must bewail with tears of compassion.
Whosoever has been victorious in battle
shall linger as if attending a memorial service.

32

TAO as the eternal is unutterable simplicity.
Even though it is small
the world dares not make it its serf.
If princes and kings could guard it in this manner
all things would come to be their guests.
Heaven and Earth would unite
to shed sweet dew.
People would find their balance
all by themselves, without orders.
When creation begins,
only then are there names.
Names too reach existence,
and one still knows where to halt.
If one knows where to halt

one is in no danger.
The relation between TAO and world
may be compared
to mountain streams and valley brooks,
that shed themselves into rivers and seas.

33

Whosoever knows others is clever.
Whosoever knows himself is wise.
Whosoever conquers others has force.
Whosoever conquers himself is strong.
Whosoever asserts himself has will-power.
Whosoever is self-sufficient is rich.
Whosoever does not lose his place has duration.
Whosoever does not perish in death lives.

34

The great TAO is overflowing:
it can be to the left and to the right.
All things owe their existence to it,
and it does not refuse itself to them.
When the work is done it does not call it its possession.
It clothes and nourishes all things
and does not play at being their master.
Inasmuch as it is forever not clamouring
one may call it small.
Inasmuch as all things depend on it

without knowing it as its master
one may call it great.

Thus also is the Man of Calling:
He never makes himself look great:
therefore he achieves the great work.

35

Whosoever holds fast to the great primal image,
to him the world will come.
It comes and is not violated:
In calmness, equity and blessedness.

Music and allurement:
They may well make the wanderer stop in his tracks.
TAO issues from the mouth,
mild and without taste.
You look for it and you see nothing special.
You listen for it and you hear nothing special.
You act according to it and you find no end.

36

What you want to compress
you must first allow truly to expand.
What you want to weaken
you must first allow to grow truly strong.
What you want to destroy

you must first allow truly to flourish.
From whomever you want to take away
to him you must first truly give.
This is called 'being clear about the invisible'.
The soft wins victory over the hard.
The weak wins victory over the strong.
One must not take the fish from the deep.
One must not show the people
the means of furthering the realm.

37

TAO is eternal without doing,
and yet nothing remains not done.
If princes and kings know how to guard it
all things will take shape by themselves.
If they take shape by themselves and desires arise
I should banish them with unutterable simplicity.
Unutterable simplicity works departure of desire.
Being without desire makes still,
and the world rights itself.

PART TWO: TE

38

Whosoever cherishes Life
does not know about Life
therefore he has Life.
Whosoever does not cherish Life
seeks not to lose Life:
therefore he has no Life.
Whosoever cherishes Life
does not act and has no designs.
Whosoever does not cherish Life
acts and has designs.
Whosoever cherishes love acts but has no designs.
Whosoever cherishes justice acts and has designs.
Whosoever cherishes morality acts
and if someone does not respond to him
he waves his arms about and pulls him up.
Therefore: If TAO is lost, then Life.
If love is lost, then justice.
If justice is lost, then mortality.
Morality is the penury of faith and trust
and the beginning of confusion.
Foreknowledge is the sham of TAO

and the beginning of folly.
Therefore the right man abides with fullness
and not with penury.
He lives in being, not in sham.
He puts the other away and adheres to this.

39

Those of old who attained the One:

Heaven attained the One and became pure.
Earth attained the One and became firm.
The Gods attained the One and became powerful.
The valley attained the One and fulfilled itself.
All things attained the One and came into existence.
Kings and princes attained the One
and became examples to the world.
All this has been effected by the One.
If Heaven were not pure through it, it would have to burst.
If Earth were not firm through it, it would have to falter.
If the gods were not powerful through it
they would have to become rigid.
If the valley were not fulfilled through it,
it would have to exhaust itself.
If things had not come into existence through it,
they would have to perish.
If kings and princes were not exalted by it,

they would have to tumble.

Therefore: The noble has the lowly for its root.
The high has the low for its foundation.

Therefore princes and kings are thus:
They call themselves 'lonely', 'orphaned', 'trifling'.
Through this they name the lowly as their root.
Is it not so?

For: without its individual parts
there is no carriage.
Do not desire the glitter of the jewel
but the raw roughness of the stone.

40

Return is the movement of TAO.
Weakness is the effect of TAO.
All things under Heaven come about in existence.
Existence comes about in non-existence.

41

If a sage of the highest order hears about TAO
he is keen to act in accordance with it.
If a sage of the middle order hears about TAO
he half believes and half doubts.
If a sage of a lower order hears about TAO
he laughs loudly about it.
If he does not laugh loudly
then it was not yet the true TAO.

Therefore the poet has these words:
'The clear TAO appears to be dark.
The TAO of progress appears as retreat.
The smooth TAO appears to be rough.
The highest Life appears as a valley.
The highest purity appears as shame.
The broad Life appears to be insufficient.
The strong Life appears to be stealthy.
The true essence appears to be changeable.
The great quadrant has no corners.
The great instrument is completed late.
The great tone has an inaudible sound.
The great image has no form.'

TAO in its seclusion has no name.
And yet it is precisely TAO
that is good at giving and completing.

42

TAO generates the One.
The One generates the Two.
The Two generates the Three.
The Three generates all things.
All things have darkness at their back
and strive towards the light,
and the flowing power gives them harmony.

What men hate
is forlornness, loneliness, being a trifle.
And yet, princes and kings
choose these to describe themselves.
For things are either increased through diminution or
diminished through increase.
I, too, teach what others teach:
'The strong do not die a natural death'.
This I will make the departure point of my teaching.

43

The softest thing on earth
overtakes the hardest thing on earth.
The non-existent overtakes even that
which has no interstices.
From this one recognises the value of non-action.
Teaching without words, the value of non-action
is attained by but few on earth.

44

Name or person:
which is closer?
Person or possession:
which is more?
Winning or losing:
which is worse?

But then:
whosoever hankers after other things
inevitably uses up the great things.
Whosoever amasses things
inevitably loses the important things.
Whosoever is self-sufficient
does not come to shame.
Whosoever knows how to practise restraint
does not get into danger
and thus can last forever.

45

Great completion must appear as if inadequate:
thus it becomes infinite in its effect.
Great abundance must appear as if flowing:
thus it becomes inexhaustible in its effect.
Great straightness must appear as if crooked.
Great talent must appear as if foolish.
Movement overcomes cold.
Stillness overcomes heat.
Purity and stillness are the world's measuring gauge.

46

When TAO rules on earth
one uses the racehorses to pull dung carts.
When TAO has been lost on earth
warhorses are raised on the green fields.

There is no greater sin than many desires
There is no greater evil than not to know sufficiency.
There is no greater defect than wanting to possess.

Therefore: the sufficiency of sufficiency is lasting sufficiency.

47

Without going outdoors
one knows the world.
Without looking out of the window
one sees the TAO of Heaven.
The further out one goes
the lesser one's knowledge becomes.

Therefore, the Man of Calling does not need to go
and yet he knows everything.
He does not need to see
and yet is he clear.
He does not need to do anything
and yet he completes.

48

Whosoever practises learning increases daily.
Whosoever practises TAO decreases daily.
He decreases and decreases
until at last he arrives at non-action.
In non-action nothing remains not done.

The realm can only be attained
if one remains free of busy-ness.
The busy are not fit
to attain the realm.

49

The Man of Calling has no heart of his own.
He makes the people's heart his own heart.
'To the good I am good;
to the non-good I am also good,
for Life is goodness.
To the faithful I am faithful;
to the unfaithful I am also faithful,
for Life is faithfulness.'
The Man of Calling lives very quietly in the world.
People look for him and listen out for him with surprise,
and the Man of Calling accepts them all as his children.

50

Going out is Life, going in is death.
Three out of ten are companions of Life.
Three out of ten are companions of death.
Three out of ten
are men who live
and thereby move towards the place of death.
What is the reason for this?
Because they want to create an increase of their lives.

I have heard that whosoever knows how to live life well
wanders through the land
and meets neither rhino nor tiger.
He walks through an army
and avoids neither armour nor weapons.
The rhino finds nothing to sink its horn into.
The tiger finds nothing to sink its claws into.
The weapon finds nothing to receive its sharpness.
Why is this so?
Because he has no mortal spot.

51

TAO generates.
Life nourishes.
Environment shapes.
Influences complete.
Therefore: all beings honour TAO
and cherish Life.
TAO is honoured,
Life is cherished,
without being outwardly appointed, just for themselves.

Therefore: TAO generates, Life nourishes,
makes grow, cares,
completes, keeps,
covers and protects.

The world has a beginning:
that is the Mother of the World.
Whosoever finds the mother
in order to know the sons;
whosoever knows the sons
and returns to the mother:
he will not be in danger all his life long.
Whosoever closes his mouth
and shuts his gates:
he will not be troubled all his life long.
Whosoever opens his mouth
and wants to set his affairs in order:
he cannot be helped all his life long.
To see the smallest means to be clear.
To guard wisdom means to be strong.
If one uses one's light
in order to return to this clarity
one does not endanger one's person.
This is called the hull of eternity.

If I really know what it means
to live in the great TAO,
then it is, above all, busy-ness
that I fear.

34 Where the great streets are beautiful and smooth

but the people prefer the sideroads;
where the rules of court are strict
but the fields are full of weeds;
where the barns are quite empty
but garments are beautiful and glamorous;
where everyone girds himself with a sharp sword;
where eating and drinking habits are refined
and goods are abundant:
there rules confusion, not government.

54

What is well planted will not be torn up.
What is well kept will not escape.
Whosoever leaves his memory to his sons and grandsons
will not fade away.
Whosoever moulds his person, his life becomes true.
Whosoever moulds his family, his life becomes complete.
Whosoever moulds his community, his life will grow.
Whosoever moulds his country, his life will become rich.
Whosoever moulds the world, his life will become broad.

Therefore: by your own person judge the person of the other.
By your own family judge the family of others.
By your community judge the community of others.
By your country judge the country of others.
By your world judge the world of others.
How do I know the nature of the world?
Just through this.

Whosoever holds fast to Life's completeness
is like a newborn infant:
Poisonous snakes do not bite it.
Scavenging animals do not lay hold of it.
Birds of prey do not hunt for it.
Its bones are weak, its sinews soft,
and yet it can grip firmly.
It does not yet know about man and woman,
and yet its blood stirs
because it has abundance of seed.
It can cry all day long
and yet its voice does not become hoarse
because it has abundance of peace.
To know peace means to be eternal.
To know eternity means to be clear.
To increase life is called happiness.
To apply one's strength to one's desire is called strong.
When things have grown strong they age.
For this is the counter-TAO,
and counter-TAO is close to the end.

He who knows does not speak.
He who speaks does not know.
One must close one's mouth
and shut one's gates,

blunt one's sharp wit,
dissolve one's confused thoughts,
moderate one's light,
make one's earthiness common.
This means hidden community with TAO.
Whosoever has this cannot be influenced by love,
nor can he be influenced by coldness.
He cannot be influenced by gain,
nor can he be influenced by loss.
He cannot be influenced by glory,
nor can he be influenced by lowliness.
Therefore is he the most glorious on earth.

57

To rule a state one needs the art of government;
for the craft of arms one needs
extraordinary talent.
But in order to win the world
one must be free of all busy-ness.
How do I know that this is the world's way?
The more things there are in the world that one must not do,
the more people are impoverished.
The more people have sharp implements,
the more house and state tumble into destruction.
The more people cultivate art and cleverness,
the more ominous signs arise.
The more law and order are propagated,
the more thieves and robbers there will be.

Therefore, the Man of Calling says:
If we do nothing
the people will change of themselves.
If we love stillness
the people right themselves of themselves.
If we undertake nothing
the people will become rich of themselves.
If we have no cravings
the people will become simple of themselves.

58

The ruler whose government is calm and unobtrusive,
his people are upright and honest.
The ruler whose government is sharp-witted and strict,
his people are underhand and unreliable.
Happiness rests on unhappiness;
unhappiness lies in wait for happiness.
But who is aware that the highest good is
not to have orders issued?
For otherwise order turns into oddities,
and good turns into superstition,
and the days of the people's delusion
are truly prolonged.

Thus also is the Man of Calling:
he sets an example without cutting others down to size;
he is conscientious without being hurtful;

he is genuine without being arbitrary;
he is bright without being blinding.

59

In leading Men and in the service of Heaven
there is nothing better than 'Limitation'.
For only through limitation
can one deal with things early on.
Through dealing with things early on
one redoubles the forces of Life.
Through these redoubled forces of Life
one rises to every occasion.
If we rise to every occasion,
no-one knows our limits.
If no-one knows our limits
we are capable of possessing the world.
If one possesses the Mother of the World
one gains eternal duration.
This is the TAO of the deep root,
of the firm ground,
of eternal existence
and of lasting sight.

60

A great country must be led
the way one fries small fish.
If one administers the world according to TAO,

then the ancestors do not swarm about as spirits.
Not that the ancestors are not spirits
but their spirits do not harm men.
Not only do the spirits not harm men,
the Man of Calling, too, does not harm them.
If then, these two powers do not harm one another,
then their Life-Forces are united in their effect.

61

By keeping itself downstream
a great realm becomes the unification of the world.
It is the female in the world.
The female always wins over the male by its stillness.
By its stillness it keeps below.
When the great realm puts itself below the small
it thereby wins the small realm over.
When the small realm puts itself below the great
it is thereby won over by the great realm.
Thus, by keeping below, the one wins over
and the other, by keeping below, is won over.
The great realm desires nothing
but to take part in the service of men.
Thus each attains what it wants:
but the great must remain below.

TAO is the homeland of all things,
the treasure of good men,
the protection of non-good men.
One may go to the market with beautiful words.
One may shine before others
with honourable conduct.
But the non-good among men—why should one throw them
away?
Therefore the ruler has been appointed
and princes have their office.
Even if one had bejewelled sceptres
to send forth in a solemn quadriga:
nothing matches the gift
which is: offering this TAO
on one's knees to the ruler.
Why did the ancients so treasure this TAO?
Is it not because it has been said of it:
'Whosoever asks will receive;
Whosoever has sinned will be forgiven'?
Therefore is TAO the most exquisite thing on earth.

Whosoever practises non-action,
occupies himself with not being occupied,
finds taste in what does not taste:
he sees the great in the small and the much in the little. 41

He repays animosity with Life.
Plan what is difficult while it is still easy!
Do the great thing while it is still small!
Everything heavy on earth begins as something light.
Everything great on earth begins as something small.
Therefore: if the Man of Calling never does anything great,
then he can complete his great deeds.
Whosoever makes promises lightly,
surely he will not keep them.
He who takes many things lightly,
surely he will have much difficulty.
Therefore: if the Man of Calling gives consideration to
    difficulties
he shall never have difficulties.

64

What is still calm can easily be grasped.
What has not yet emerged can easily be considered.
What is still fragile can easily be broken.
What is still small can easily be scattered.
One must work on what is not yet there.
One must put in order what is not yet confused.
A tree trunk the size of a fathom
grows from a blade as thin as a hair.
A tower nine stories high
is built from a small heap of earth.
A journey of a thousand miles
starts in front of your feet.

Whosoever acts spoils it.
Whosoever keeps loses it.

Thus also is the Man of Calling:
He does not act, thus he spoils nothing.
He does not keep, thus he loses nothing.
People go after their affairs,
and always when they have nearly finished
they spoil it.
Pay attention to the end as much as to the beginning:
then nothing will be spoiled.

Thus also is the Man of Calling:
He desires desirelessness.
He does not desire goods that are hard to attain.
He learns non-learning.
He turns back to that which the multitude passes by.
Thereby he furthers the natural course of things
and does not dare to act.

65

Those of old who were competent
in ruling according to TAO
did not do it by enlightening the people
but by keeping the people unknowing.
The difficulty in leading the people
comes from their knowing too much.

Therefore: whosoever leads the state through knowledge
is the robber of the state.
Whosoever does not lead the state through knowledge
is the good fortune of the state.
Whosoever knows these two things has an ideal.
Always to know this ideal is hidden Life.
Hidden Life is deep, far-reaching,
different from all things,
but in the end it works the great success.

66

Rivers and seas are the kings of the streams
because they know how to keep themselves below.
Therefore are they the kings of the streams.

Thus also is the Man of Calling:
if he wants to stand above his people
he puts himself below them in speaking.
If he wants to be ahead of his people
he stands back.
Thus also:
He dwells in the high place
and the people are not burdened with him.
He stays in the prime place
and the people are not hurt by him.
Thus also:
the whole world is willing to advance him

and does not grow unwilling.

Because he does not quarrel
no-one in the world can quarrel with him.

67

All the world says that my TAO may be great
but, in a manner of speaking, useless.
Just because it is great,
therefore it is, in a manner of speaking, useless.
If it were useful
it would long ago have grown small.
I have three treasures
that I treasure and guard.
The first is called 'love';
the second is called 'sufficiency';
the third is called 'not daring to lead the world'.
Through love one may be courageous,
through sufficiency one may be generous.
If one does not dare to lead the world
one may be the head of complete men.
If one wants to be courageous without love,
if one wants to be generous without sufficiency,
if one wants to advance without standing back:
that means death.
If one has love in battle
one is victorious.
If one has it in defence
one is invincible.

Whom Heaven wants to save
him he protects through love.

68

Whosoever knows how to lead well
is not warlike.
Whosoever knows how to fight well
is not angry.
Whosoever knows how to conquer enemies
does not fight them.
Whosoever knows how to use men well
keeps himself below.
This is the Life that does not quarrel;
this is the power of using men;
this is the pole that reaches up to Heaven.

69

Among soldiers there is a saying:
I dare not play the lord and master,
I'd rather play the guest.
I dare not advance an inch,
I'd rather withdraw a foot.
This means walking without legs,
fighting without arms.

There is no greater misfortune
than underestimating the enemy.

If I underestimate the enemy

I am in danger of losing my treasure.
Where two armies confront each other in battle
the conqueror will be he who wins with a heavy heart.

70

My words are very easy to understand
and easy to carry out.
But no-one on earth can understand them
nor carry them out.
Words have an ancestor.
Deeds have a lord.
Because they are not understood
I am not understood.
It is precisely in being so rarely understood
that my value rests.
Therefore the Man of Calling
walks in haircloth
but in his bosom he guards a jewel.

71

To know non-knowledge
is the highest good.
Not to know what knowledge is
is a kind of suffering.
Only if one suffers from this suffering
does one become free of suffering.
If the Man of Calling does not suffer

it is because he suffers of this suffering:
therefore he does not suffer.

72

When people do not fear what is terrible,
then the great terror comes.
Do not make their dwellings narrow
nor their life vexed.
For it is because of this—
that they do not live in narrowness—
that their life does not become vexed.

Thus also is the Man of Calling:
He knows himself but does not want to shine.
He loves himself but does not seek honour for himself.
He removes the other and takes this.

73

Whosoever shows courage in daredevilry
will perish.
Whosoever shows courage without daredevilry
will stay alive.
Of these two the one brings gain,
the other harm.
However, who knows the reason
why Heaven hates one?

Thus also is the Man of Calling:
He sees the difficulties.
The TAO of Heaven does not quarrel
and yet has the gifts necessary to be victorious.
He does not speak
and yet he finds the right answer.
He does not beckon
and yet everything comes of itself.
He is tranquil
and yet is he competent in planning.
Heaven's nets are wide-meshed
but they lose nothing.

74

If the people do not fear death:
how can one frighten them with death?
But if I keep the people constantly
in fear of death and
if someone does strange things:
should I grab him and kill him?
Who dares do this?
There is always a power of death that kills.
To kill instead of leaving killing to this power of death
is as if one wanted to use the axe oneself
instead of leaving it to the carpenter.
Whosoever would use the axe
instead of leaving it to the carpenter

shall rarely get away
without injuring his hand.

75

When the people go hungry,
this comes from too much tax
being devoured by the high and mighty:
therefore the people go hungry.
When the people are hard to lead,
this comes from too much meddling
by the high and mighty:
therefore are they difficult to lead.
When the people take death too lightly,
this comes from life's abundance being sought too greedily
by the high and mighty:
therefore do they take death too lightly.
However, he who does not act for the sake of life,
he is better than the other to whom life is precious.

76

Man, when he enters life,
is soft and weak.
When he dies
he is hard and strong.
Plants, when they enter life,
are soft and tender.
50 When they die

they are dry and stiff.
Therefore: the hard and the strong
are companions of death;
the soft and the weak
are companions of life.

Therefore: when weapons are strong they are not victorious.
When trees are strong they are cut down.
The strong, the great, is below.
The soft, the weak, is above.

77

The TAO of Heaven: how it resembles the archer!
He presses down what is high
and raises that which is low.
Whatever has too much he reduces,
whatever does not have enough he completes.
It is the TAO of Heaven
to reduce what has too much
and to complete what does not have enough.
Man's TAO is not so.
He reduces what does not have enough,
in order to offer it to what has too much.
But who is capable of offering to the world
that of which he has too much?
Only he who has TAO.

Thus also is the Man of Calling:
he works and does not keep.

When the work is done he does not tarry with it.
He does not desire to show off his importance to others.

78

In the whole world there is nothing softer
and weaker than water.
And yet nothing measures up to it
in the way it works upon that which is hard.
Nothing can change it.
Everyone on earth knows
that the weak conquers the strong
and the soft conquers the hard—
but no-one is capable of acting accordingly.

Thus also spoke the Man of Calling:
'Whosoever takes upon himself the filth of the realm,
he is the lord at the earth's sacrifices.
Whosoever takes upon himself the misfortune of the realm,
he is the king of the world.'
True words are as if contrary.

79

If one placates great anger
and yet there remains anger:
how could this be good?
Therefore the Man of Calling adheres to his duty

and demands nothing of others.

Therefore: whosoever has Life
adheres to his duty;
whosoever does not have Life
adheres to his right.

80

A country shall be small
and its populace small in number.
Implements that multiply men's strength
shall not be used.
People are to take death seriously
and shall not travel far away.
Even though there be ships and carriages
no-one shall travel in them.
Even though there be armour and weapons
no-one shall employ them.
Let the people tie knots in ropes
and use them instead of script.
Make their food sweet
and their garments beautiful,
their dwellings peaceful
and their customs joyful.
Neighbouring countries may be within eyesight
so that one can hear the cocks crow and the dogs bark
on either side.
And yet shall people die at great age
without having travelled hither and thither.

True words are not beautiful,
beautiful words are not true.
Competence does not persuade,
persuasion is not competent.
The sage is not learned,
the learned man is not wise.
The Man of Calling does not heap up possessions.
The more he does for others,
the more he possesses.
The more he gives to others,
the more he has.
The TAO of Heaven is 'furthering without causing harm'.
The TAO of the Man of Calling is to be effective without
quarrelling.